This Book Belongs To:

....

....

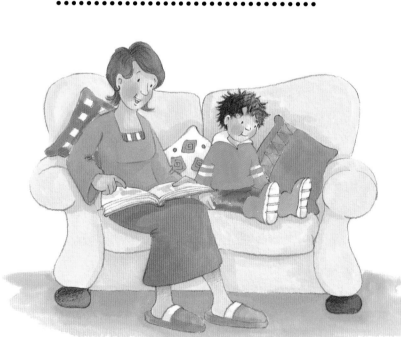

Stories for Two Year Olds

Stories for **Two** Year Olds

Parragon

Bath • New York • Singapore • Hong Kong • Cologne • Delhi
Melbourne • Amsterdam • Johannesburg • Auckland • Shenzhen

Illustrated by Alison Atkins

First published by Parragon in 2011

Parragon
Queen Street House
4 Queen Street
Bath BA1 1HE, UK

Copyright © Parragon Books Ltd 2003

ISBN 978-1-4454-1986-2

Printed in China

Contents

Teddy Goes Flying

Every day, Teddy played in the backyard with Joe.

One morning, Joe accidentally dropped Teddy into a puddle. Joe went rushing inside to tell Mom.

"Don't worry, Joe," said Mom. "We'll put Teddy in the washing machine with the towels. He'll be clean again soon."

Teddy went round and round in the washing machine. The soap bubbles washed away all the mud. Soon Teddy was nice and clean.

Swish, swish, swish!

Then Mom hung Teddy out to dry on the clothes line while she and Joe went shopping.

Suddenly, the wind blew Teddy off the line.

Teddy swept and swooped over rooftops and yards. He soared, glided, dipped, and flipped. He had never had so much fun!

"Whee!" Teddy called. "I'm flying!"

Teddy flew down over one garden where there were swings and a slide.

"Joe and I could have so much fun playing there!" he thought.

Suddenly, the wind started to drop. Teddy fell all the way down to the ground, and…**SPLASH!** into another big puddle, right in front of Joe's house.

"It's Teddy!" cried Joe, running ahead as they returned home. "He's wet and muddy again!"

"We'll have to throw him back into the washing machine," said Mom.

Suddenly the wind picked up.

"Only this time," she added, "I think we'll put him in the dryer!"

"Good idea," said Joe.

"A very good idea!" thought Teddy.

Ben's Boots

Ben really loved his shiny blue boots. When it rained, he would **splash** in the puddles on his way to preschool.

Even when it was hot, Ben would wear his blue boots!

One morning Ben found it hard to put his boots on. Mom said he should get some new ones as he'd gotten too big for them.

"I don't want new ones," said Ben at once.

"You can't wear boots that are too small, Ben," said Mom. "They'll hurt your feet."

The lady at the shoe store didn't have any blue boots in Ben's size.

"You'll have to try these yellow ones on, Ben," Mom said. "They look really good."

"No they don't!" thought Ben. "I won't wear them!"

At home,
Ben tugged and
pulled his old
boots on. Then he
went into the kitchen
for dinner. Mom saw
the boots, and smiled.

"Okay," she said.
"You can wear your
blue boots for
one last time."

Ben wore
them all through
story time after dinner.

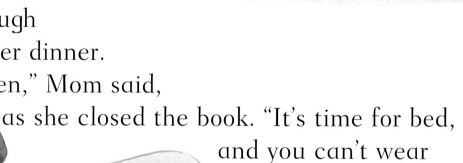

"Okay, Ben," Mom said,
as she closed the book. "It's time for bed,
and you can't wear
boots in bed."

"Yes I can,"
said Ben, running
up the stairs
and jumping
into bed.

Ben grabbed his favorite teddy bear and held him tight.

And that was when Mom had an idea.

"Poor Teddy," she said. "I thought he could have your blue boots, Ben, so he could come out with you to play when it's wet."

"Oh!" said Ben. This was really hard. He couldn't keep his old boots if Teddy needed them, could he? And it would be great to take Teddy out in the rain with him.

Ben tugged off his blue boots. He slipped them onto Teddy's feet.

Mom handed the yellow boots to Ben. He slipped them on and lifted his feet up to show Teddy. "Ben's boots!" he said proudly.

Jack and the Mice

Jack was Katy Cat's kitten.

"I'm going to teach you about mice," Katy Cat said to Jack. "It's our job to catch them."

Jack liked catching things, so this sounded fun.

At the other end of the backyard, Mitzi Mouse and her children, Miles and Melanie, came out of their nest.

"I want you to look for food," she told them, "but you must watch out for cats!"

"What's a cat?" asked Miles and Melanie together.

"Cats are very dangerous creatures," their mother explained. "They move very fast, but you must move faster!"

Miles and Melanie both nodded. "We will, Mom," they promised.

A little while later, Jack was sniffing all around and twitching his whiskers as he looked around for mice.

Not far away, Miles and Melanie went out to look for food, with their whiskers wiggling and their tails twittering.

Jack saw the two little creatures running through the grass.

"Are you mice?" Jack asked them.

"Y-yes," said Miles, nervously.

"Are you a cat?" asked Melanie.

"Yes," said Jack. "I think I'm supposed to catch you, but I'd rather play."

So Jack, Miles, and Melanie began to play together.

The three friends were right in the middle of a wonderful game of tag when Katy Cat looked up and saw Jack chasing Miles and Melanie.

At that Moment, Mitzi Mouse came out of her nest and saw her children running away from Jack.

As Miles and Melanie ran away, Jack padded back to his mom, who was happy to see him chasing mice.

And on the other side of the yard, Mitzi Mouse was glad to see her children escape from the cat.

Jack looked back at Miles and Melanie.

All three winked, then gave a little wave with their tails and twitched their whiskers. It was their way of letting each other know they'd be back again tomorrow —to have lots more fun together!

Backstroke Benny

Mama Duck looked at her four new ducklings, Benny, Kenny, Jenny, and Penny. She wanted them to become strong swimmers, so the ducklings practiced flapping their feet every day.

"Get ready for your first swim, my dears!" she told her ducklings one day. "Line up behind me."

"Now," said Mama Duck, when everyone was in the water, "stay right behind me, flap your feet, and—

SWIM!"

The little ducklings followed behind Mama Duck
—all except Benny, who was going the wrong way!

"You're doing the backstroke," called Mama Duck.
"You need to flap your feet forward!"

Benny tried to flap his feet forward, but they
wouldn't go. He just went backward faster.

"It's no use!" he called. "I can only swim
backward!"

Benny's family tried to help, but no matter
what they did, Benny could only swim one way—
backward!

As they swam along the lake, Jenny, Penny, and Kenny told Benny what they could see up ahead, and Benny told them what he could see happening behind them.

"A fox is coming out of the trees and two rabbits are running away," said Benny.

"A fox?" said his brother and sisters.

"A FOX!" quacked Mama Duck. "Quick! We have to get away!"

"Follow me!" said Benny, swimming to the front of the line. Doing the backstroke, Benny guided his family away from the fox.

When the fox was gone, everyone breathed a sigh of relief. Then they gathered round Benny.

"Benny, your backstroke saved the day," said Mama Duck. "Three cheers for Backstroke Benny!"

As everyone cheered, Mama Duck watched proudly.

"I knew all my ducklings would be fine swimmers," she thought, "but even I didn't know just how special Backstroke Benny would be!"

Jasmine's Summer Lullaby

One warm summer's night, Jasmine just could not get to sleep. The next day was her birthday and she was very excited.

"What I really need is someone to sing me a lullaby," she muttered to herself.

A small bird outside Jasmine's bedroom window heard this and sang to her. Then her cat and dog tried to join in!

But it didn't make Jasmine sleepy.

Soon, Mom came in to see what all the noise was about.

"I can't sleep," said Jasmine.

"Well, I'll sing you the lullaby my mother sang to me," said Mom. "It always put me to sleep."

Jasmine snuggled up against her mom to listen.

Mom gently began to sing a soft lullaby. Soon, all the animals began to join in with her mother's singing.

The sound was so restful that in no time at all Jasmine was fast asleep. **ZZZZZZZZZZZ!**

Her mother quietly stopped singing, and tucked the covers around Jasmine's chin. She then put a little present on the pillow by Jasmine's head.

"Something for you to open when you wake up, Jasmine," she whispered. "Now, come along you animals, time for us all to go to sleep."

Soon all of the animals had dozed off happily too.

In the morning, Jasmine spotted the present Mom had left on her pillow.

"Ooh, a birthday present!" she cried, unwrapping it excitedly. Inside the bright wrapping paper was a little music box. When Jasmine opened the lid, the box played the tune that her mother had sung to her the night before.

"Now I can get to sleep whenever I want to," said Jasmine happily and, from then on, she always could.